Pat and

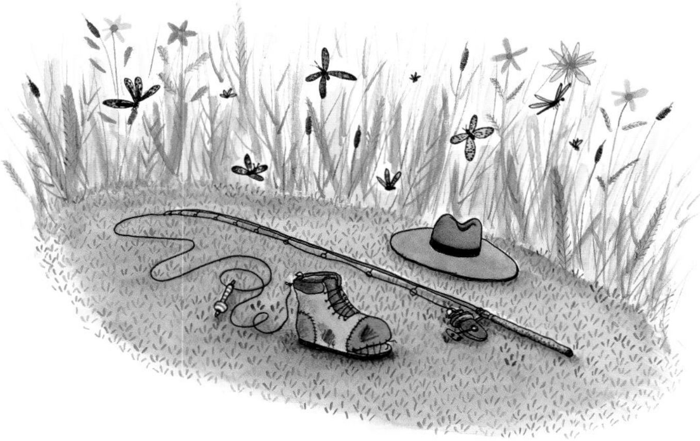

Monica Hughes
Illustrated by Matt Buckingham

RIGBY

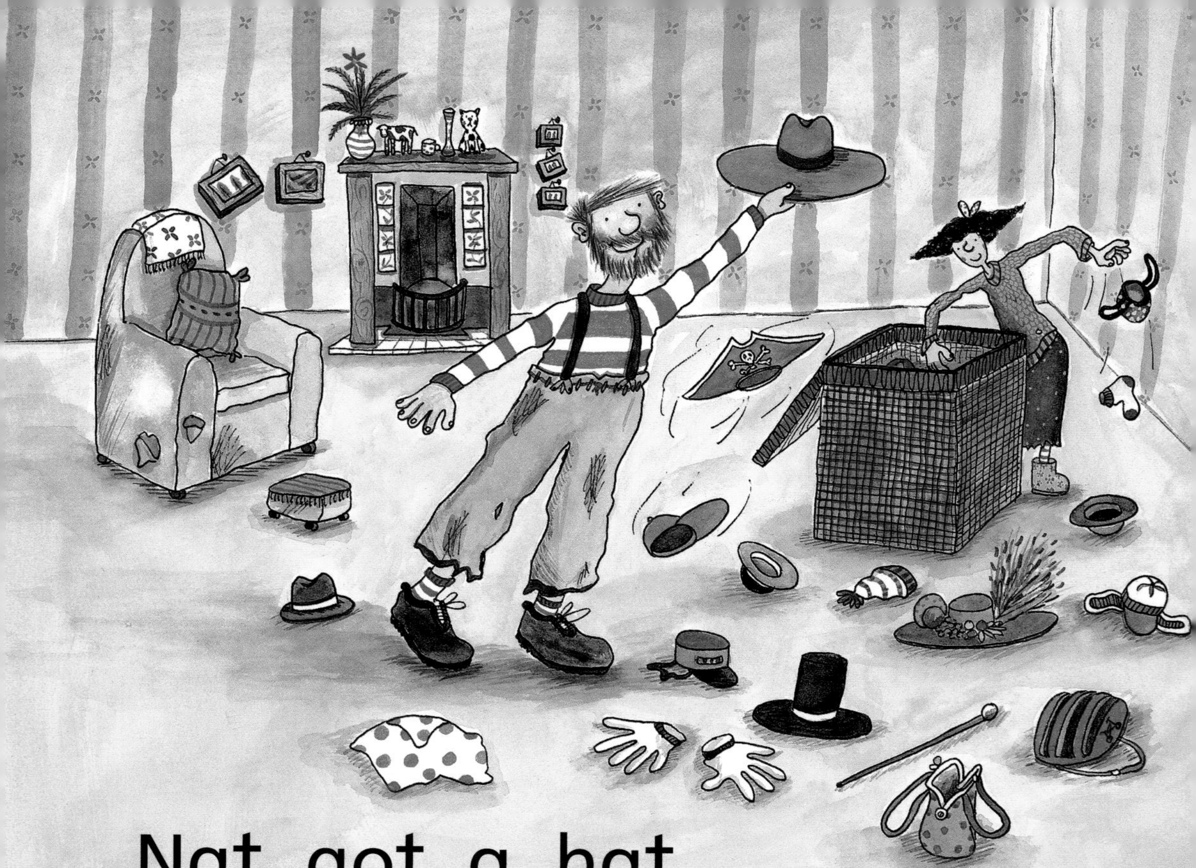

Nat got a hat.

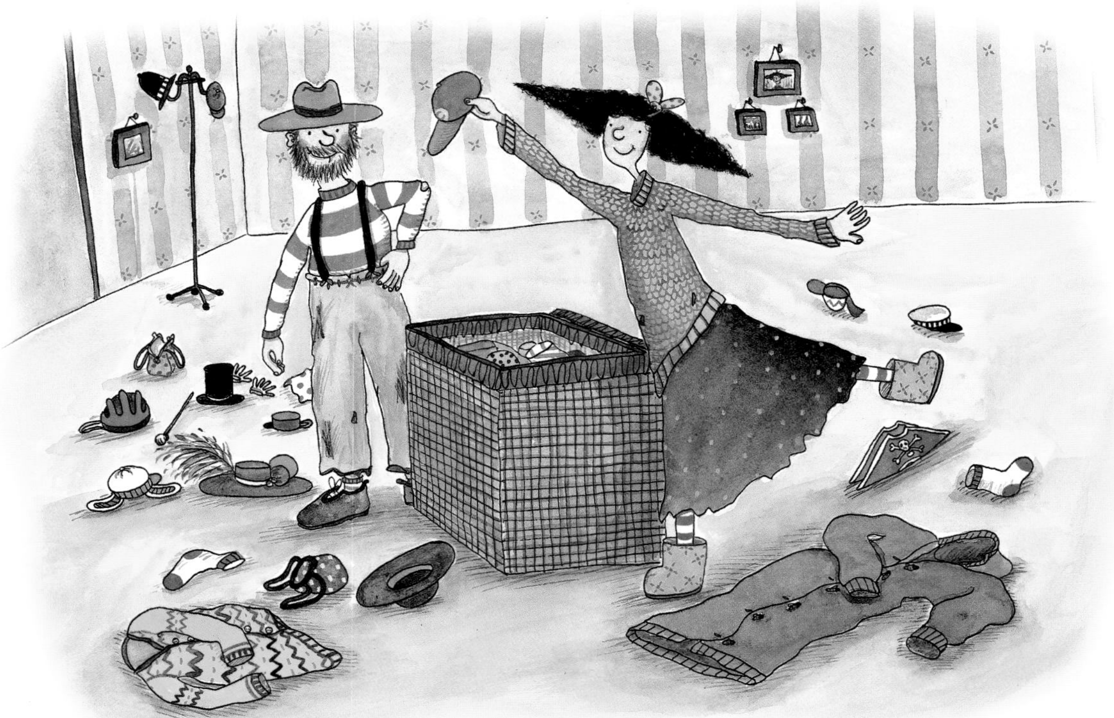

Pat got a cap.

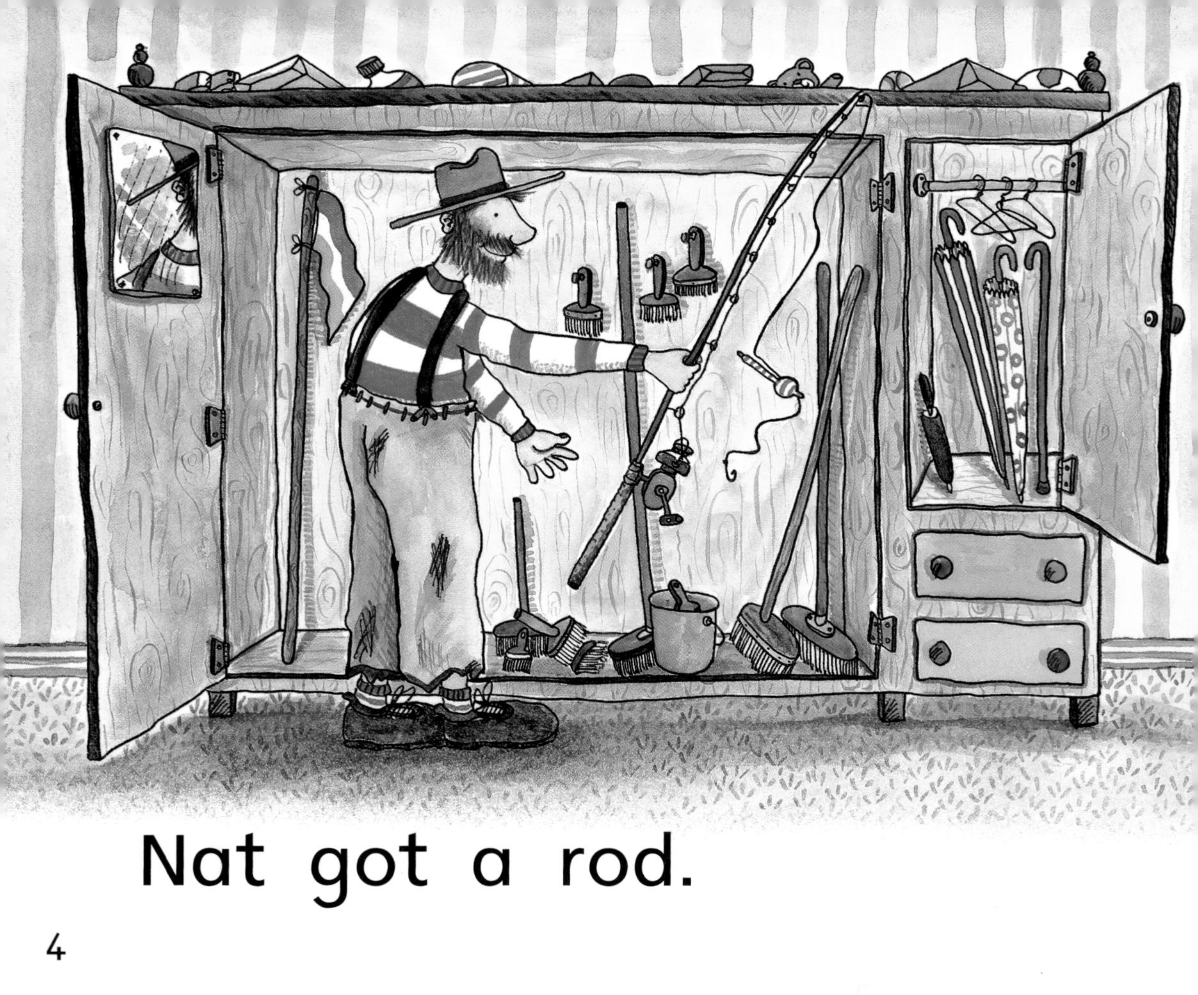

Nat got a rod.

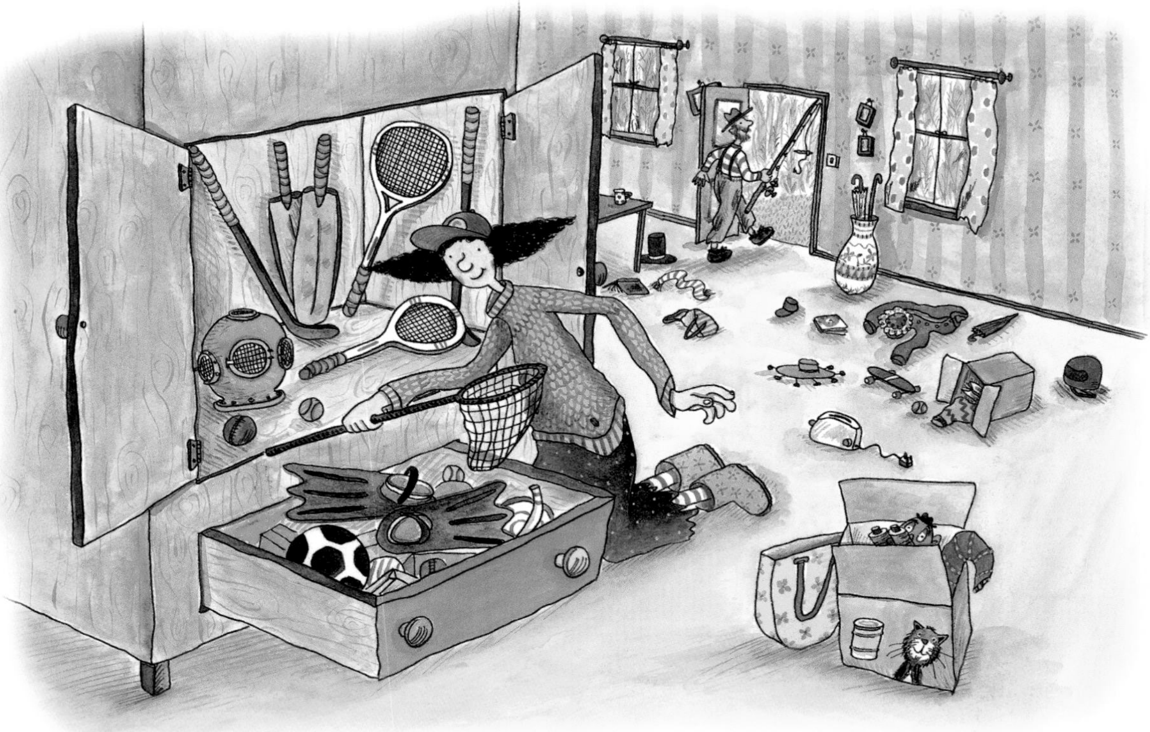

Pat got a net.

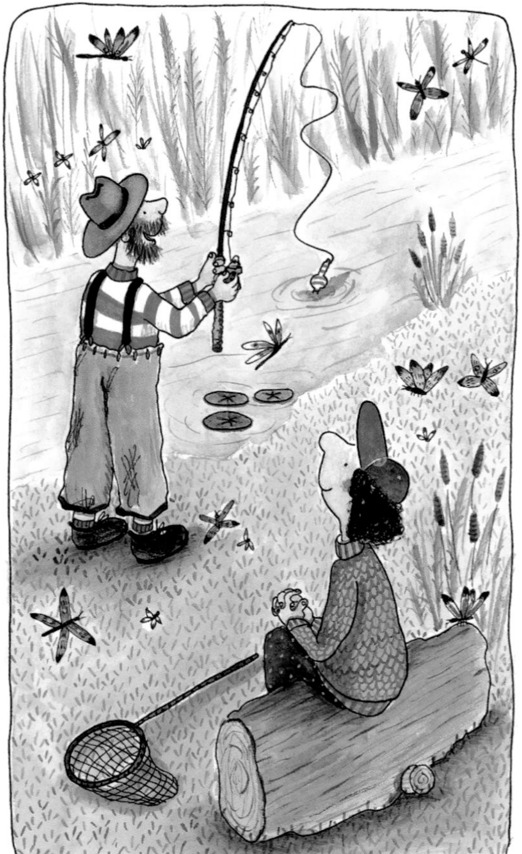

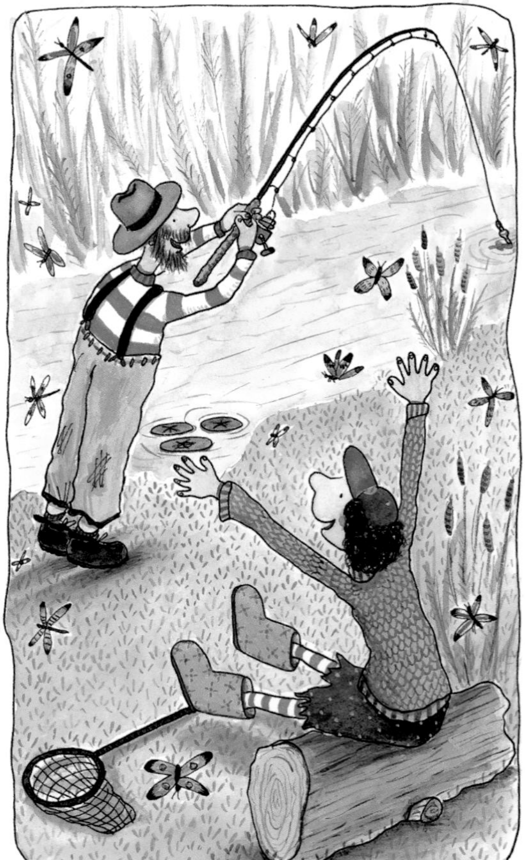

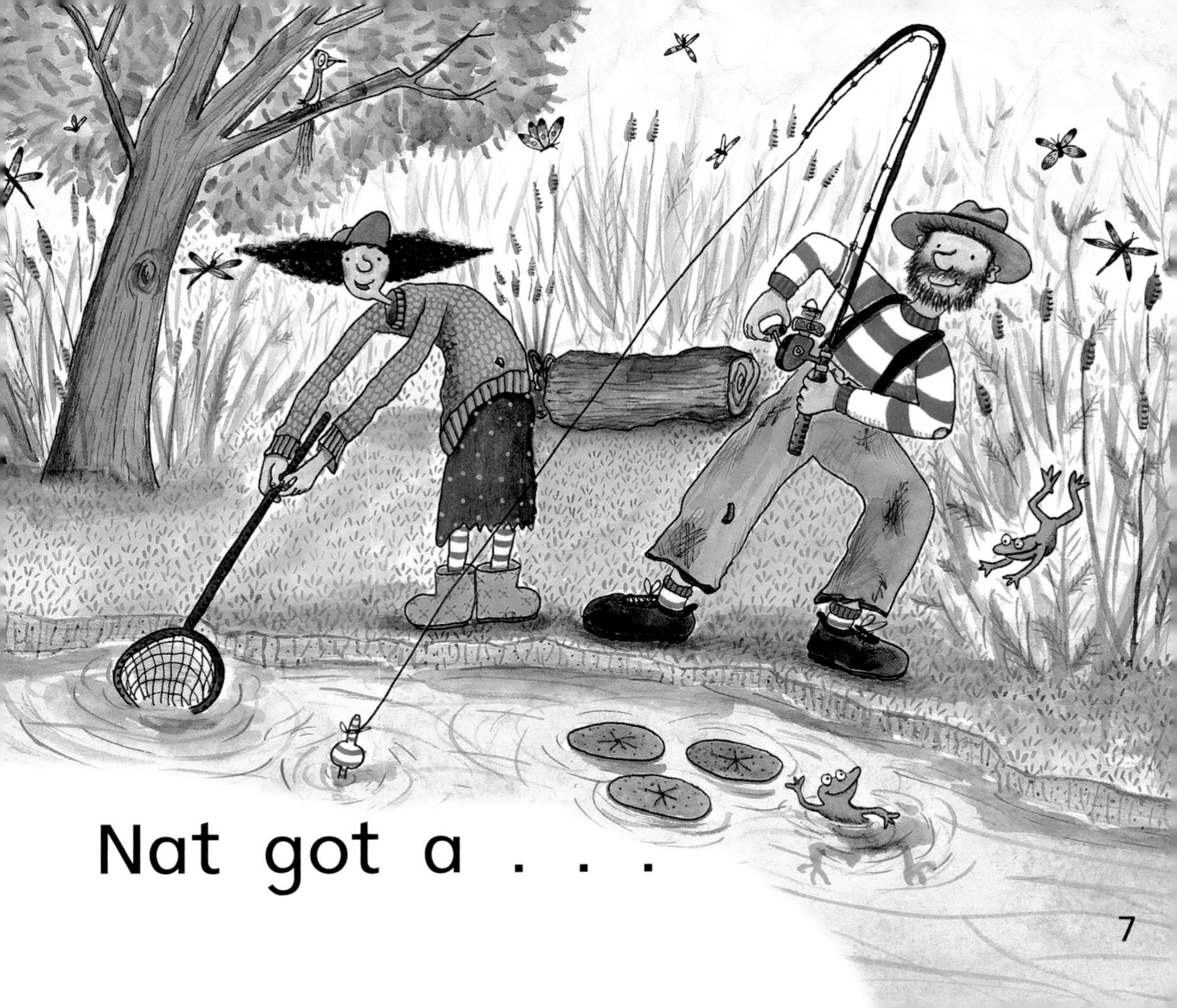

Nat got a . . .

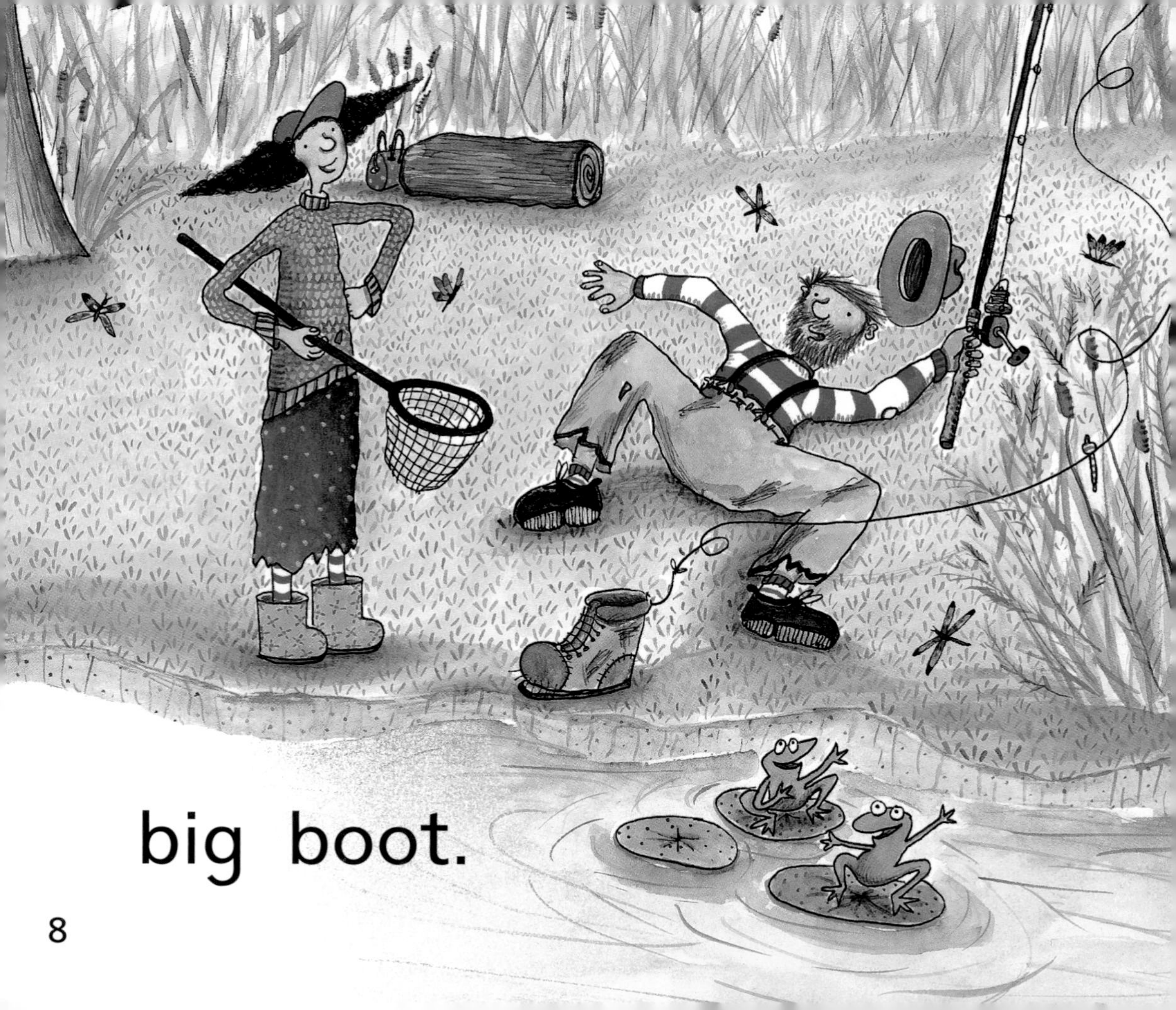

big boot.